SPEED MACHINES

FERRARI

Julia J. Quinlan

PowerKiDS press

New York

Published in 2013 by The Rosen Publishing Group, Inc.
29 East 21st Street, New York, NY 10010

First Edition

Editor: Jennifer Way
Book Design: Greg Tucker

Photo Credits: Cover, pp. 9, 25 Oksana.Perkins/Shutterstock.com; p. 4 © www.iStockphoto.com/Sjoerd van der Wal; p. 5 Dongliu/Shutterstock.com; p. 6 © National Motor Museum/age fotostock; p. 7 (top) Thomas D. McAvoy/Time & Life Pictures/Getty Images; p. 7 (bottom) Car Culture/Getty Images; p. 8 Radim Drtilek/Shutterstock.com; p. 10 Ben Smith/Shutterstock.com; pp. 11 (top), 20 Max Earey/Shutterstock.com; p. 11 (bottom) Massimiliano Lamagna/Shutterstock.com; p. 12 David Acosta Allely/Shutterstock.com; pp. 13, 26 Natursports/Shutterstock.com; p. 14 cjmac/Shutterstock.com; p. 15 Ahmad Faizal Yahya/Shutterstock.com; pp. 16–17 © Hans Dieter Seufert/c/age fotostock; pp. 18, 23 EvrenKalinbacak/Shutterstock.com; p. 19 (top) Faiz Zaki/Shutterstock.com; p. 19 (bottom) esbobeldijk/Shutterstock.com; p. 21 Natali Glado/Shutterstock.com; p. 22 karlstury/Shutterstock.com; p. 24 Mike Fanous/Gamma-Rapho/Getty Images; p. 27 Fedor Selivanov/Shutterstock.com; p. 28 hfng/Shutterstock.com; p. 29 Francesco Dazzi/Shutterstock.com.

Library of Congress Cataloging-in-Publication Data

Quinlan, Julia J.
 Ferrari / by Julia J. Quinlan. — 1st ed.
   p. cm. — (Speed machines)
 Includes index.
 ISBN 978-1-4488-7457-6 (library binding) — ISBN 978-1-4488-7529-0 (pbk.) —
 ISBN 978-1-4488-7604-4 (6-pack)
 1. Ferrari automobile—Juvenile literature. I. Title.
 TL215.F47Q56 2013
 629.222—dc23
                              2012002897

Manufactured in the United States of America

CPSIA Compliance Information: Batch #B4S12PK: For Further Information contact Rosen Publishing, New York, New York at 1-800-237-9932

Contents

The Flashy Ferrari

Ferraris have been among the most desired cars in the world since the 1940s. Ferrari is known for its eye-catching, fast cars. Ferrari began as a racecar company. Those beginnings are felt in its sports cars. Ferrari is famous for its sports cars with 12-**cylinder** engines. These are also known as V12 engines. Most road cars have engines with four or six cylinders. The extra cylinders in Ferraris' engines make the cars roar

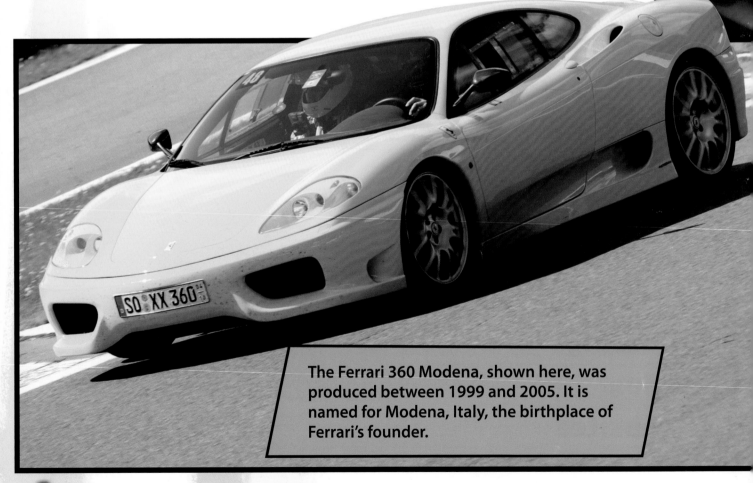

The Ferrari 360 Modena, shown here, was produced between 1999 and 2005. It is named for Modena, Italy, the birthplace of Ferrari's founder.

Novitec Rosso, a company that makes changes to cars to improve their performance, has made this Ferrari even more powerful.

as they **accelerate** with great power. This makes drivers feel as though they are speeding around a racetrack when they are really just driving down regular roads!

Ferrari has been making sports cars since 1947 and racecars since 1929. Ferrari does not make very many of each car. People who want one usually have to sign up on a waiting list! People are willing to wait for the latest models and to pay a huge price for them.

Beginnings in Italy

    Enzo Anselmo Ferrari was the founder of Ferrari. He was born in Modena, Italy, in 1898. Ferrari loved cars from an early age and wanted to grow up to be a racecar driver. He was also interested in the mechanical side of how cars worked. He wanted to build cars as well as race them.

    In 1920, Ferrari began working for Alfa Romeo, an Italian car company. Eventually, Ferrari left Alfa Romeo and created his own company, Ferrari S.p.A. Ferrari's new company made both racecars and road cars. Ferrari S.p.A

Here is the 125 Sport, or 125 S, Ferrari's first racecar.

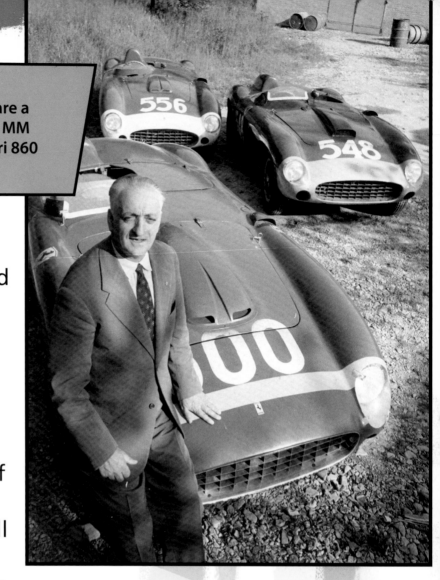

Enzo Ferrari is shown here posing with three racecars in 1956. They are a Ferrari 290 MM (front), Ferrari 290 MM Scaglietti (back right), and a Ferrari 860 Monza Scaglietti (back left).

made its first racecar, called the 125 Sport, in 1947. Ferrari made its first true road car in 1949. It was called the 166 Inter. Enzo Ferrari's love of racecars can be seen in both the design and performance of every model from the 125 Sport to today's models. All Ferraris accelerate quickly and have **precise** handling, just as a racecar does.

This Ferrari 166 from 1947 is one of the first cars built by Ferrari.

Racecar Inspirations

Ferraris are known for their speed and the control the driver can have on the car while moving quickly. Ferraris are made for people who enjoy driving long distances and who like to feel as though they are driving racecars. Ferraris are also known for being handmade. They are put together by hand rather than by machines, as most other cars are.

The Ferrari Enzo's engine, shown here, is a V12 engine.

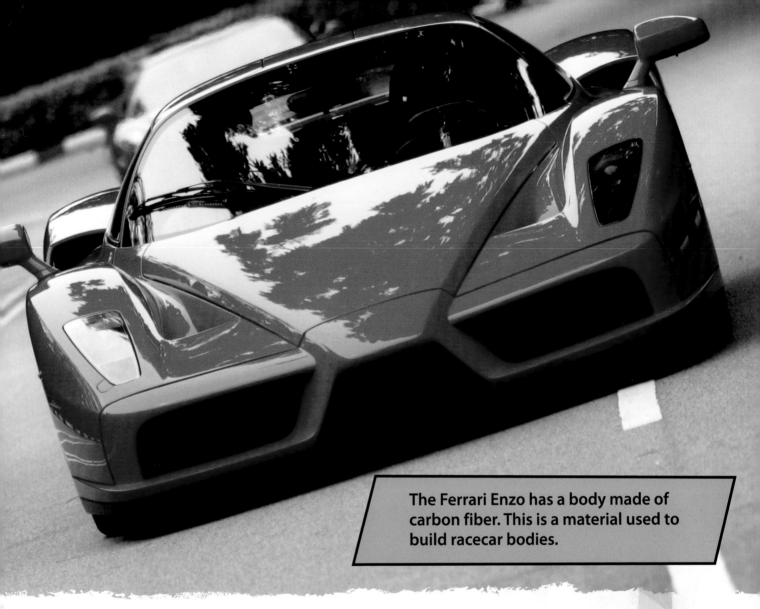

The Ferrari Enzo has a body made of carbon fiber. This is a material used to build racecar bodies.

Many Ferraris have 12-cylinder engines that make a roaring sound as they are driven. Most Ferraris can go over 200 miles per hour (322 km/h). Ferraris come in many colors, but they are known for being bright red. The logo for Ferrari is a leaping black stallion on a yellow background. Ferraris are often designed to look sleek and **aerodynamic**. Ferrari uses design companies to create the looks of their cars. Pininfarina is one of the main car-design companies that works with Ferrari.

Sports Cars

Ferrari sports cars are stylish and powerful. Ferrari is known for making cars with 12-cylinder engines, but it also makes sports cars with 8-cylinder engines. The 458 Italia and California models have V8 engines. The Ferrari Four and the 599 GTO have V12 engines. Ferrari is currently making six models of grand tourers. They are the 458 Italia, California, Ferrari Four, 599 GTO, and the 458 Spider. Ferrari also has a special limited-edition model called the SA Aperta. Grand tourers, usually

The convertible version of a sports car, like this F430, is called a Spider.

Above: Racing versions of some Ferraris, like the 458 shown here, are used in long races called endurance races. *Below*: The Ferrari 430 goes from 0 to 60 miles per hour (0–97 km/h) in 4 seconds!

shortened to "GTs," are luxury sports cars that are made for long-distance driving. Most GTs have two doors. All of the current models have top speeds of 200 miles per hour (322 km/h) or more.

One of the most recognizable Ferrari models is the Testarossa. The Testarossa is no longer made but was extremely popular in the 1980s and 1990s.

Racecars

The first car built by Ferrari, the 125 S, was a racecar. Only two of the cars were made. The 125 S was driven in 14 races and won 6. Racecars are built differently from sports cars. They are made only for racing. They are not made to be driven on regular streets. They are extremely fast and aerodynamic. It is important for racecars to be able to take sharp turns and to accelerate quickly. Ferrari races in Formula One races. Formula One racecars are specially designed for racing and have only one seat, for the driver.

If a car is aerodynamic, it means that air flows around the car without slowing it down. The force of air slowing down a car is called drag.

This is a Ferrari 150° Italia racecar. The suspension on a racecar is tight. This gives a bumpy ride but helps the driver feel the road.

Since 1947, there have been 57 Ferrari racecars. Ferrari makes new racecars almost every year. Every year, these new cars are lighter, faster, and safer. The 2011 racecar is called the Ferrari 150° Italia. Before the 150°, Ferrari named its cars after the year they were built. The 2010 racecar was called the F10.

Formula One Champions

Ferrari has competed in Formula One races since its beginnings. Formula One cars are the fastest racecars in the world. They race at speeds of up to 220 miles per hour (354 km/h). Formula One teams race in a series of races around the world called Grands Prix. Teams earn points based on how they finish in the Grand Prix races. The higher they finish, the more points they earn. The team with the most points at the end of the season is the champion.

Scuderia Ferrari is Italian for "team Ferrari." Its literal meaning is "Ferrari stable." This name refers to the horse on the company's logo.

Here is driver Fernando Alonso racing for Scuderia Ferrari in 2011.

Ferrari's racing team is called Scuderia Ferrari. Scuderia Ferrari has competed since 1932. It is the oldest Grand Prix racing team. Scuderia Ferrari holds many records. It has the most constructor championships, with 16. "Constructor" means that the team made its own car. It also holds the record for most driver championships, with 15.

In 2012, the team had two main drivers. They were Fernando Alonso and Felipe Massa. There was one backup driver named Jules Bianchi.

Testarossa

The Ferrari Testarossa is one of Ferrari's most recognizable cars. *Testarossa* means "redhead" in Italian. The car is the bright red that Ferrari is known for. It was introduced at the 1984 Paris Motor Show. It replaced an earlier model, the 512 BBi.

The Testarossa was made from 1984 until 1996. It was extremely popular and 9,957 were sold during its production years. The Testarossa has a 380-horsepower, 12-cylinder engine. The car has a five-speed manual **transmission**. It can go from 0 to 60 miles per hour (0–97 km/h) in 5.3 seconds. Its top speed is 175 miles per hour (282 km/h). The Testarossa was wider and more angular than earlier Ferrari models. Its futuristic design, created by the Pininfarina design house, was hated by some but loved by many.

The vents along the Testarossa's doors are called strakes. They help make the car more aerodynamic.

Testarossa

Engine size	4.9 liters
Number of cylinders	12
Transmission	Manual (stick shift)
Gearbox	5 speeds
0–60 mph (0–97 km/h)	5.3 seconds
Top speed	175 mph (282 km/h)

458 Italia

Ferrari unveiled the 458 Italia in 2009, at the Frankfurt Motor Show. The car has a 4.5-liter V8 engine, with 570 horsepower and 400 pounds-feet of **torque**. The 458 can reach 60 miles per hour (97 km/h) in 3.4 seconds and has a top speed of 202 miles per hour (325 km/h). Ferrari used a wind tunnel to design the car so the designers could see how air would pass around the car when it was moving. By using a wind tunnel, they were able to make the car have less **drag** as it

Here is a 458 Italia at a 2010 car show in Istanbul, Turkey.

458 Italia

Engine size	4.5 liters
Number of cylinders	8
Transmission	Semiautomatic (dual clutch)
Gearbox	7 speeds
0–60 mph (0–97 km/h)	3.4 seconds
Top speed	202 mph (325 km/h)

Top: The 458 Italia has three exhaust pipes. *Bottom*: This is the racing version of the 458 Italia.

was moving. The 458 Italia also has a seven-speed dual-clutch transmission, which lowers the car's carbon dioxide **emissions** and fuel **consumption**.

The 458 Italia was recalled in September 2010 after several of the cars burst into flames. This was because of a design flaw. One of the glues used in the car was **flammable**. Ferrari replaced or repaired the cars.

Ferrari Four

The Ferrari Four, or FF, has four seats and is the first Ferrari to have four-wheel drive. This means all four wheels are powered by the engine, giving the driver great control of the car. The FF's four-wheel drive is different from traditional all-wheel drive. Ferrari **patented** this system in 2005. The Ferrari Four was introduced at the Geneva Motor Show in 2011. The FF replaced the 612 Scaglietti.

The 612 Scaglietti, shown here, was produced between 2004 and 2011.

Ferrari Four

Engine size	6.3 liters
Number of cylinders	12
Transmission	Semiautomatic (dual clutch)
Gearbox	7 speeds
0–60 mph (0–97 km/h)	3.7 seconds
Top speed	208 mph (335 km/h)

Ferrari says that the FF is the world's fastest four-seat car.

The Ferrari Four takes only 3.7 seconds to reach 60 miles per hour (97 km/h) and has a top speed of 208 miles per hour (335 km/h). It has a 651-horsepower engine. Unlike many Ferraris, the Ferrari Four has a trunk with room for luggage and groceries. It is the first car with a 12-cylinder engine to have a seven-speed, dual-clutch gearbox. This is a transmission that has two clutches and that can be run either as a manual or an automatic transmission.

California

The Ferrari California, introduced in 2008, was inspired by the Ferrari 250 California. The 250 California was released in 1957 and was one of the most popular early Ferrari models. The modern Ferrari California comes only as a convertible. It was the first Ferrari model to have a **retractable** folding metal hardtop roof.

The California has two front seats and the option to add up to two additional seats in the back. It is slightly less powerful than other Ferraris, with only

The California's hardtop roof folds into the car's body. This is how a cloth-top convertible top works, but the hardtop stands up to bad weather better.

California

Engine size	4.3 liters
Number of cylinders	8
Transmission	Semiautomatic (dual clutch)
Gearbox	7 speeds
0–60 mph (0–97 km/h)	3.8 seconds
Top speed	193 mph (311 km/h)

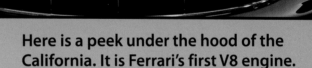

Here is a peek under the hood of the California. It is Ferrari's first V8 engine.

450 horsepower and a top speed of 193 miles per hour (311 km/h). This makes it a little more practical for everyday driving. It is still able to accelerate very quickly, though. It can reach 60 miles per hour (97 km/h) in just 3.8 seconds.

Enzo

The Enzo was introduced in 2002. The name was chosen because the car was released shortly after what would have been the one-hundredth birthday of Enzo Ferrari and also the fiftieth anniversary of the company. The Enzo is inspired by Formula One racecars. The interior of the car is very simple, with all of the control buttons around the steering wheel, just as they are in a racecar.

One of the 399 Ferrari Enzos produced was painted a special color called *rosso Dino* or "Dino red." Dino was the name of Enzo Ferrari's son who died as a young man.

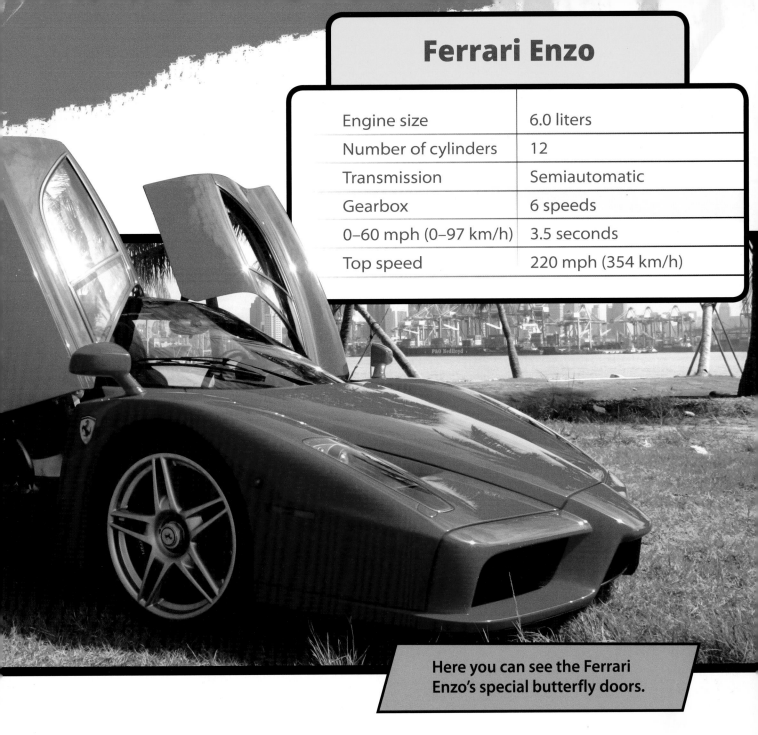

Ferrari Enzo

Engine size	6.0 liters
Number of cylinders	12
Transmission	Semiautomatic
Gearbox	6 speeds
0–60 mph (0–97 km/h)	3.5 seconds
Top speed	220 mph (354 km/h)

Here you can see the Ferrari Enzo's special butterfly doors.

The Enzo has a V12 engine and has 650 horsepower. It can reach 60 miles per hour (97 km/h) in just 3.5 seconds and can go up to 220 miles per hour (354 km/h). The Enzo has special doors, called butterfly doors. They open out and up, as opposed to regular doors, which open only out. When the Enzo first came out, it sold for more than $650,000. Now that it is out of production, it can be sold at auction for up to $1 million!

150° Italia

The Ferrari 150° Italia is the current model of Ferrari used by its Formula One race team, Scuderia Ferrari. The car is named in honor of the 150th anniversary of Italy becoming a country. The Ferrari 150° is the fifty-seventh racecar built by Ferrari for Formula One racing. It replaced the older model, the F10. The Ferrari 150° has a V8 engine that weighs 209 pounds (95 kg). The car weighs 1,411 pounds (640 kg). This is much lighter than most road cars. Ferrari updates its racecars frequently because

Here is the Ferrari 150° Italia during a race in Barcelona, Spain, in 2011.

150° Italia

Engine size	2.3 liters
Number of cylinders	8
Transmission	Semiautomatic
Gearbox	7 speeds
Top speed	180 mph (290 km/h)

This is the driver's seat in the Ferrari 150° Italia. The driver's seat in a racecar is called the cockpit.

Formula One changes requirements for cars regularly. The 150° Italia was made to be safer than the previous model.

The 150° was originally called the F150, but its name was changed after Ford threatened to sue Ferrari. F150 was the name of a Ford truck before it was the name of the Ferrari racecar.

Ferrari Today and in the Future

In 2010, Ferrari introduced the HY-KERS experimental vehicle. The HY-KERS is Ferrari's first **hybrid** vehicle. It has an electric motor and a V12 gas-powered engine. Drivers will be able to switch between the electric motor and the V12 engine, depending on what they need at the time. For driving around town, the electric motor

The Ferrari 599 HY-KERS is expected to be in production by 2015.

The 599XX is the racing version of the 599 GTB Fiorano.

is enough. For longer, faster drives, the V12 engine works better. The HY-KERS is bright green instead of the bright red of most Ferraris. This is because Ferrari is "going green," or trying to make some cars that burn less gas, which is kinder to the environment.

Ferrari continues to be one of the most popular makers of sports cars in the world. In the first half of 2011, Ferrari had already sold 3,577 cars. Ferraris are most popular in North America. The Ferrari Four was so popular that it was sold out as of 2012!

Comparing Ferraris

CAR	YEARS MADE	SALES	TOP SPEED	FACT
Testarossa	1984–1996	9,957	175 mph (282 km/h)	The Testarossa was designed to be the successor to the Ferrari Berlinetta Boxer.
458 Italia	2010–	1,248	202 mph (325 km/h)	The 458 Spider is the convertible version of this car.
FF	2011–	800	208 mph (335 km/h)	The FF's body style is called shooting brake.
California	2008–	3,023	193 mph (311 km/h)	Ferrari made another California in the 1950s called the 250 GT California Spider.
Enzo	2002–2004	400	220 mph (354 km/h)	*Sports Car International* magazine named the Enzo one of the top sports cars of the 2000s.
150° Italia	2011–	n/a	220 mph (354 km/h)	This car won the 2011 British Grand Prix.

Glossary

accelerate (ik-SEH-luh-rayt) To increase in speed.

aerodynamic (er-oh-dy-NA-mik) Made to move through the air easily.

consumption (kun-SUMP-shun) The act of using something.

cylinder (SIH-len-der) The enclosed space for a piston in an engine.

drag (DRAG) A force that goes against the motion of an object as the object tries to move through a gas, such as air, or a liquid.

emissions (ee-MIH-shunz) Things, such as pollution or gases, put into the air by something, such as an engine.

flammable (FLA-muh-bel) Can easily burn.

hybrid (HY-brud) Having an engine that runs on gasoline and a motor that runs on electricity.

patented (PA-tent-ed) Had a document that stops people from copying an invention.

precise (prih-SYS) Exact.

retractable (rih-TRAK-tuh-bel) Can be drawn back.

torque (TORK) The force from a car's engine that produces rotation in the drive shaft.

transmission (trans-MIH-shun) A group of parts that includes the gears for changing speeds and that conveys the power from the engine to the machine's rear wheel.

Index

Websites

Due to the changing nature of Internet links, PowerKids Press has developed an online list of websites related to the subject of this book. This site is updated regularly. Please use this link to access the list: www.powerkidslinks.com/smach/fer/